Many Days, One Shabbat

BY **Fran Manushkin**

ILLUSTRATED BY **Maria Monescillo**

Marshall Cavendish Children

Text copyright © 2011 by Fran Manushkin
Illustrations copyright © 2011 by Maria Monescillo

All rights reserved
Marshall Cavendish Corporation, 99 White Plains Road, Tarrytown, NY 10591
www.marshallcavendish.us/kids

Library of Congress Cataloging-in-Publication Data

Manushkin, Fran.
Many days, one shabbat / by Fran Manushkin ; illustrated by Maria
Monescillo. — 1st Marshall Cavendish Shofar bk. ed.
p. cm.
Summary: A family prepares for and celebrates shabbat.
ISBN 978-0-7614-5965-1 (hardcover)   ISBN 978-0-7614-6080-0 (ebook)
[1. Sabbath—Fiction. 2. Jews—Fiction.] I. Monescillo, Maria, ill. II.
Title.

PZ7.M3195Man 2011
[E]—dc22
2011001126

The illustrations are rendered in watercolor, textures, and digital retouching.
Book design by Anahid Hamparian
Editor: Margery Cuyler

Printed in China (E)
First edition
10 9 8 7 6 5 4 3 2 1

Marshall Cavendish
Children

SHOFAR BOOKS

JEWISH BEDTIME STORIES & SONGS FOR FAMILIES

The PJ Library is an international, award-winning program created by the
Harold Grinspoon Foundation to support families on their Jewish journeys.
To learn more about The PJ Library, visit www.pjlibrary.org.

For Ellie, Max, Ian, and Alex Adler—F. M.

To my sister Ana who has many ways
and one dream—M. M.

One morning.
Many kisses.

One house.
Many rooms.

One flower.
Many petals.

One person.
Many fingers.

One box.
Many colors.

One shirt.
Many buttons.

One car.
Many people.

One match.
Many candles.

One challah.
Many slices.

One sky.
Many stars.

One good night.
Many kisses!

Shabbat Shalom!